Ole Könnecke

ANTON
AND THE
BATTLE

GECKO PRESS

First American edition published in 2013 by Gecko Press USA, an imprint of Gecko Press Ltd.
A catalog record for this book is available from the US Library of Congress.

Distributed in the United States and Canada by Lerner Publishing Group, Inc.
241 First Avenue North, Minneapolis, MN 55401 USA
www.lernerbooks.com

Distributed in the UK by Bounce Sales and Marketing

This edition first published in 2013 by Gecko Press
PO Box 9335, Marion Square, Wellington 6141, New Zealand
info@geckopress.com

English language edition © Gecko Press Ltd 2013

Original title: Anton und der große Streit
By Ole Könnecke
© Carl Hanser Verlag München 2012

A catalogue record for this book is available from the National Library of New Zealand.

Translated by Catherine Chidgey
Edited by Penelope Todd
Typesetting by Luke Kelly, New Zealand
Printed by Everbest, China

ISBN hardback 978-1-877579-26-4
ISBN paperback 978-1-877579-25-7

For more curiously good books, visit **www.geckopress.com**

Here comes Anton.

And here comes Luke.

"I'm stronger than you," says Anton.
"Very funny!" says Luke.

"I can lift a stone this big," says Anton.
"Is that all?" says Luke.

"I can lift a stone THIS big!"
"I'm still stronger than you," says Anton.

"I can carry three logs at once!"
says Anton. "No sweat."

"Bah," says Luke.

"I can carry a whole piano.
I'm much stronger than you.

AND MUCH, MUCH LOUDER!"

"I'm even louder than you!" says Anton.

"Louder! Louder! Louder!!!"

"I'll blow you away!" shouts Luke.

"I'll flatten you!" shouts Anton.

"I'll blow you up!"

"Dare you! Dare you!"

"I'll drop a bomb THIS BIG on your head!"

"Don't care! My bomb's bigger!
I'm stronger!"

"No way! I can swing a man-eating tiger over my head!"
"Who cares? I can do it with a lion. Ha!"

"I can slay a four-headed dragon!"
"So can I! So can I!"

Uh-oh! There's a dog.

Woof!

Woof!

A big dog.

Woof!

"Go away!" shouts Anton.
"Get lost!" shouts Luke.

But the dog won't go.

Woof?

"I want to go home," says Anton.
"I'm hungry," says Luke.
"I'm much hungrier than you," says Anton.

Woof!

"I could eat a cake this big!" says Anton.
"I could eat one THIS big!" says Luke.

"I'd drink a glass of juice this big," says Anton.
"Well, I'd drink one THIS big. With a huge straw!"

"Look, the dog's gone."
"We can go home!"

"I'm fast," says Anton.
"I'm faster!" says Luke.